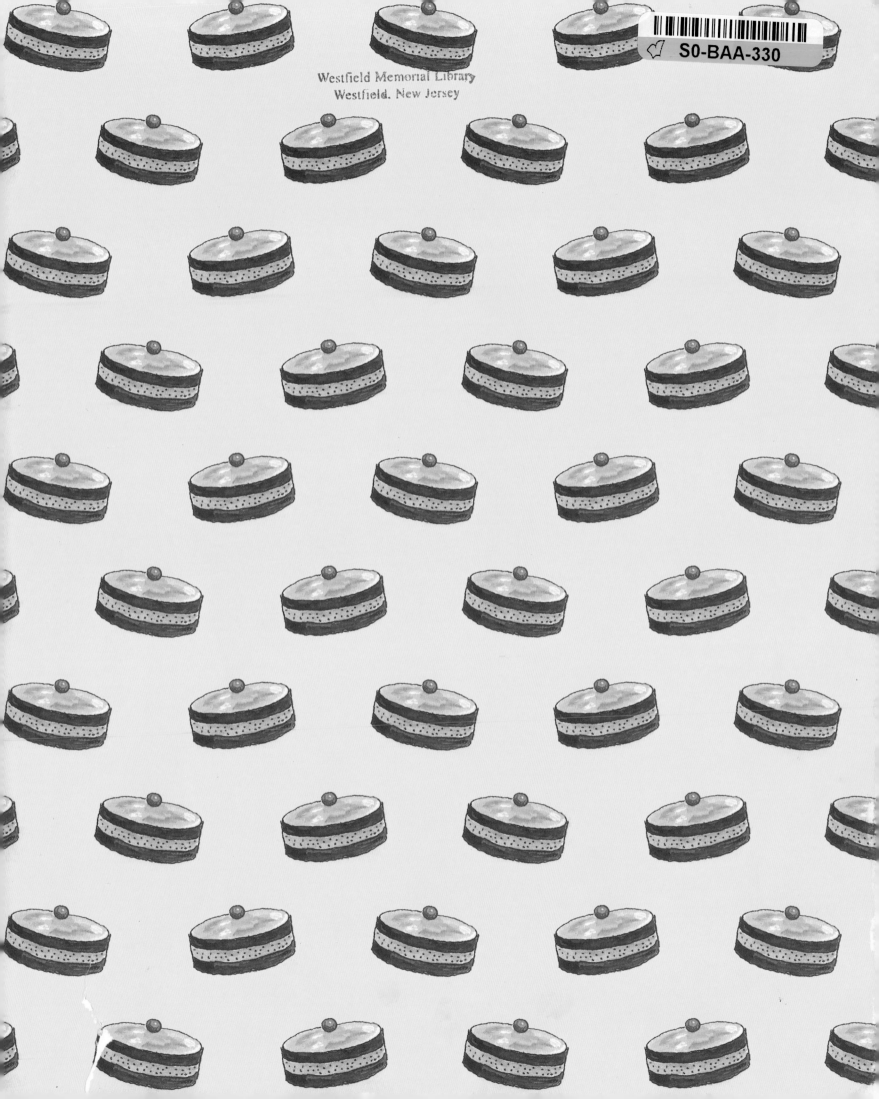

For Kim, Pim, Lis, Tobias, Nicci, Jonathan, and Emma

Illustrations copyright © 2004, Thé Tjong-Khing

Original edition © 2004, Uitgeverij Lannoo nv, Tielt, www.lannoo.com

Original title: *Waar is de Taart?* Translated from the Dutch language

English translation © 2007, Harry N. Abrams, Inc.

Library of Congress Control Number: 2006926330
ISBN 13: 978-0-8109-1798-9
ISBN 10: 0-8109-1798-X

Printed and bound in Hong Kong
10 9 8 7 6 5 4 3 2 1

HNA ▮▮▮▮▮
harry n. abrams, inc.
a subsidiary of La Martinière Groupe
115 West 18th Street
New York, NY 10011
www.hnabooks.com

Where Is the Cake?

T. T. Khing

Abrams Books for Young Readers
New York